Eagle's Reflection

and Other Northwest Coast Stories

Learning from Nature and the World Around Us

Robert James Challenger

Heritage House Publishing Company Ltd.
#108 – 17665 66A Avenue
Surrey, BC V3S 2A7
www.heritagehouse.ca

Library and Archives Canada Cataloguing in Publication
Challenger, Robert James, 1953–
    Eagle's Reflection and Other Northwest Coast Stories

ISBN 978-1-895811-07-0

    1. Nature Stories, Canadian (English)*.   2. Children's stories, Canadian (English)*   I. Title

PS8555.H34E33 1996   jc813'.54   C95-910680-4
PZ7.C52Ea 1996

All illustrations: Robert James Challenger
Book design and layout: Cecilia Hirczy Welsford
Editor: Rhonda Bailey

Printed in Canada

Heritage House acknowledges the financial support for its publishing program from the Government of Canada through the Book Publishing Industry Development Program (BPIDP), Canada Council for the Arts, and the province of British Columbia through the British Columbia Arts Council and the Book Publishing Tax Credit.

The Canada Council | Le Conseil des Arts
for the Arts | du Canada

BRITISH
COLUMBIA
ARTS COUNCIL
We acknowledge the support of the Province of British Columbia
through the British Columbia Arts Council

Dedicated

to

my family, my friends,

and our world.

Other books by Robert James Challenger

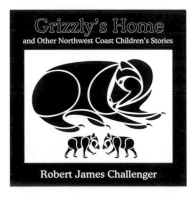

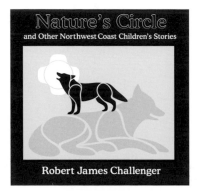

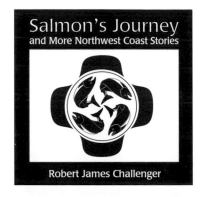

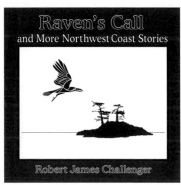

Grizzly's Home
and Other Northwest Coast Children's Stories
ISBN 978-1-894384-94-0

Nature's Circle
and Other Northwest Coast Children's Stories
ISBN 978-1-894384-77-3

Salmon's Journey
and More Northwest Coast Stories
ISBN 978-1-894384-34-6

Raven's Call
and More Northwest Coast Stories
ISBN 978-1-895811-91-9

Orca's Family
and More Northwest Coast Stories
ISBN 978-1-895811-39-1

All $9.95

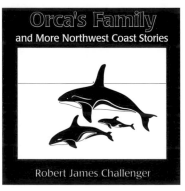

Wonderful Northwest Coast stories for kids … Jim Challenger is a real artist as his book demonstrates.

—Ron MacIssac, Shaw Cable's "What's Happening?"

I really loved your stories that you read to us. I really got the feeling of what you meant in your magical writing. Thank you for coming to our school to make us feel joyful. I enjoyed your stories!! Sincerely,

—Josey L. (Age 8)

Modern day fables are the right length. … knows how to write for the oral storyteller; the written words slip easily off the tongue.

—*Times Colonist*

Challenger's prose bears a deliberate resemblance to First Nations oral traditions: humans and nature interact freely, and both are capable of folly, repentance, and wisdom. In his artwork, Challenger also embraces West Coast Aboriginal culture by portraying his characters in exquisite Haida-style prints. Highly recommended.

—Steve Pitt, *Canadian Book Review Annual*

Contents

Nature Lessons

Eagle soared high in the summer sky above the green trees. He was watching the village on the other side of the forest.

Eagle was worried because many of the people who lived there had chosen to ignore Nature's lessons. They did not respect their world or the other plants and creatures that lived within it. Instead of living in harmony, they fought with other people and destroyed the forests, birds, animals and fish. Friends abandoned them, and wood and food became harder to find. As time passed, each day became more miserable than the one before. But instead of changing, these people continued to abuse the few remaining gifts Nature had given.

Eagle flew to a place where people had made different choices. There, people used the forest wisely, never taking more than it could offer. They respected the other people, fish, birds, and animals and made sure they all had a home. For these people life was good, for as they took care of Nature, Nature took care of them.

Eagle flew down and called to them, "Across the forest is a place where people are destroying all that Nature has given them. We must help them before it is too late." With that he transformed the people into magical animals, fish and birds and led them to the other village.

They began to teach the people about Nature's ways and show them there are both good and bad choices. They taught them that if they choose not to honour the forest and animals around them, then Nature will take those gifts away. If they choose to respect the world around them, Nature will take care of them forever.

At first the people did not believe them. It was hard not to take all the wood and food when they were cold and hungry. But the people began to try, and slowly their world changed. The forest began to grow back and the birds, fish and animals started to return.

It was difficult to do, and the people had just begun to learn. That is why today Eagle still soars over the forest, watching carefully to see that they continue to respect Nature's lessons.

Bear's Gift

The campfire crackled and gave warmth to the old man and children gathered around it. Beyond the light of the fire the forest was dark and full of shadows.

One of the children said, "I'm glad you are here, Grandfather, because you are big and strong like Bear. You can protect us from wild animals."

The old man placed a log on the fire and as the sparks flew into the night sky he said, "Well, Bear was not always the great beast we know today. When Bear first came to the forest he was small—so small the other animals and birds did not even notice him.

"But one day when Bear was wandering in the forest, he came upon Raven lying on the ground. Raven was hurt and could not fly. Bear did not know what to do. He was not big enough to lift Raven and take him to safety.

"Raven said to him, 'If I make you strong, will you help me?'

"Bear was not sure how Raven could do that, but he said, 'Yes, I will take care of you.'

"Raven touched Bear's back and immediately huge muscles bulged beneath the fur. Bear used his new strength to pick up Raven and carry him back to his den. As he had promised, Bear took care of him until Raven could fly again.

"Before Raven left, he said to Bear, 'You have been a good friend. From now on, every time you help someone you will grow bigger, stronger and more respected.'"

The old man stopped to place another log on the fire. Then he said, "Bear has helped many others through the years and that is why he is now the biggest, strongest and most respected animal in our forest."

Grandfather smiled at the children gathered around him and said, "Bear started small and grew with each good thing he did. He did not use his strength to scare others; instead he used it to help them. In turn, they gave him all the respect he deserved.

"As you grow up, remember the story of Bear. Know that true respect comes only as a gift from others."

Hummingbird

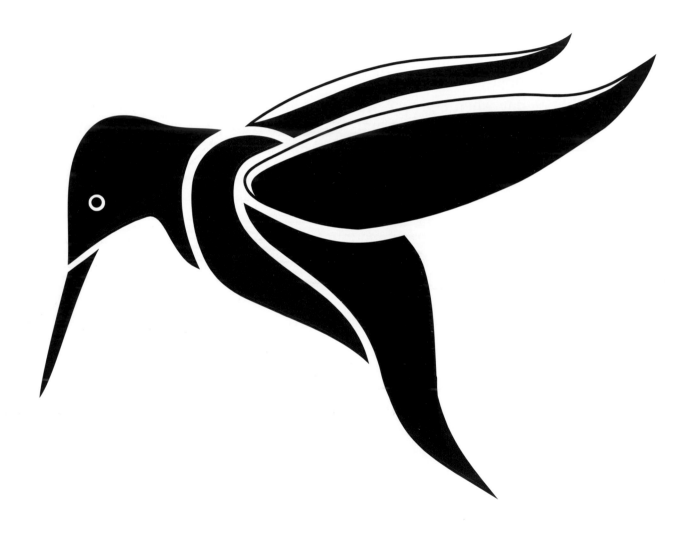

It was a warm, spring day. Summer was coming and the wildflowers were in full blossom. A young girl and her mother waded through the green grass, enjoying the bright colors. They stopped as Hummingbird joined them, buzzing and darting from flower to flower.

The child was fascinated by the little creature. She asked, "Why does such a tiny bird want to fly so fast? Why doesn't it just stay at one flower instead of visiting every one?"

Her mother sat down on a hill overlooking the field and said, "Let me tell you the story of Hummingbird."

"Many years ago there was a fragrant flower that rose every spring to display her beautiful petals and bright colours for all the world's creatures to enjoy. The people and animals waited anxiously each spring for this special flower to appear. On that day they knew the warm, kind days of summer had arrived.

"Raven saw how much joy this flower brought to the world, so the next spring when it appeared, he transformed it into a tiny bird. The bird had the colours of the green spring grass and the flashing red of a setting sun. Raven gave the bird a special gift—to fly like sunlight flickering through tall trees. He also gave it a message to take to all the flowers.

"That's why today we see Hummingbird buzzing from flower to flower, whispering a message. Hummingbird is thanking each flower for making our world a more beautiful place."

The mother looked at her child and said, "As you grow up, remember that like each flower, each person has gifts to give to the world. In return that person will be thanked by the birds, animals and flowers for helping to make our world a better place for everyone."

Eagle's Reflection

On the ocean shoreline an evening campfire flickered as the family sat reflecting on the day just passed and anticipating the one to come.

Grandfather spoke. "We are all at different places on the journey along life's path," he said. "Some have barely started, others are well on their way; some like me, are nearing its end. Along the way I have been challenged many times to decide on the right path to take."

His grandchild asked, "How did you choose?"

The old man answered, "When I was not sure, I looked to the sky to see which way Eagle flew. It seemed when I followed the noble path of Eagle, I would find true happiness and contentment. Although that path was often steeper, narrower, and more challenging, Eagle watched over it and helped those who followed him.

"Now that I am old and look back, I see those who chose another path. As the journey lengthened, their way became ever more difficult. One wrong turn led to another and, without Eagle as their guide, they were all eventually lost and forgotten."

He stopped, looked around at his family, and said, "Our lives mirror the path each of us chooses to follow. Those of you who take the noble path will have lives that give back good fortune and admiration, just like Eagle. Those who do not will have lives that reflect all the wrong they have done.

"Remember, when Eagle looks down at the still water, his reflection is that of a noble bird. If you choose right over wrong, then when you look into still water the reflection you see will be that of a noble person."

Heron

Everyone was busy. People were caring for their families—searching for food, preparing warm clothes, and gathering wood for their winter fire. Nobody seemed to pause, even for a moment, though it was a beautiful summer evening. None took time to see the eagle soaring overhead, the salmon jumping in the bay, or the otter loping along the beach.

Raven watched an old man sitting on a beach log observing all the activity. She knew the man was already looking forward to morning when he would steal away from the village before dawn and spend time on the far shore of the bay, quietly fishing in the still water.

Raven flew down to the log and landed near the man. Raven said to him, "You're a wise fellow. You have found a balance between busy and quiet time. Other people are missing the best things offered to them each day because their lives are too complicated and full of tasks."

Raven decided to give the man a gift. "I am giving you a special power to turn anyone into a graceful Heron. Then they can learn, like you have, the joy and contentment that comes from standing in the early dawn, listening to the silence, being alone with your thoughts, and taking time to reflect on life around you. As the daylight grows, they will transform back into their human form, but will take those lessons with them."

Ever since then, at each dawn we see Heron wading in the shallow, calm water. The sun rises and splashes the shore. Streaks of warm light dance around the graceful, quiet bird. Heron reminds us to find a peaceful balance in our own lives, and to take time to watch and enjoy the world around us.

Coho Learns to Jump

On a cold winter night, a young boy sat in a carving shed watching his grandfather work on a totem pole. The boy asked, "Grandfather, how did you learn to carve such a big log?"

Grandfather smiled and sat down with his grandson by the warm fire. "Let me tell you the story of Coho salmon. That will help you find the answer to your question.

"Coho was born in the river. When he was very young, just like you, he swam down the river into the ocean. Along his journey he watched others and learned from them. He also learned from his own mistakes and successes. Soon he knew when to use his strength and when to use his knowledge to survive.

"Coho liked to try things, so one day he decided to see what was above the ocean waves. He swam straight up and shot through the surface of the water into the air. Coho felt the warmth of the sun on his scales; he saw the birds in the sky and the animals on the land. But all too soon he fell back into the sea. He did not give up. He practiced his jumps, each one getting higher and longer, until he could jump almost to the sky itself.

"When Coho grew old, like me, he returned to the river where he was born, but it had changed. Wind had toppled an old tree across the channel, blocking the way for all the salmon. But Coho knew how to get past. He showed the other salmon how to jump. One by one they swam up the river, leapt into the air and landed on the other side of the log. When all the fish were past the log, Coho went on to the place of his birth where he helped spawn the next generation of salmon."

Grandfather paused for a moment and picked up a small piece of wood. He smiled and said, "That is why on calm days out on the ocean we see salmon practicing their jumps, so they will not be stopped by any obstacles on their journey."

Grandfather handed the boy a chisel and the small piece of wood. "Watch me and learn from what I do. Practise, and learn from your mistakes. Do not give up just because your first try is not successful. That way, you will know what to do when you reach the big log and begin carving it into your own totem pole."

Kingfisher

A family walked together along the beach as waves rolled up onto the sand and gulls screeched overhead. Sunlight flashed through the trees; the air was fresh with the smell of fall.

The oldest child was restless. She often spoke of leaving home but kept changing her mind. Grandmother took her aside and they sat on a log looking out over the sparkling sea.

Grandmother said, "It is not an easy choice you have to make. Leaving home to start out on your own is a big step. Perhaps the story of Kingfisher will help you decide."

She took her granddaughter's hand: "Long ago there was a young man, about your age, who was supposed to go out each day and catch fish for his family. But he had a problem making decisions. He thought about going fishing in the early morning, but by the time he made up his mind it was already noon. He considered going later in the day, but it was dark before he decided. If he did go fishing, he seldom stopped paddling to let down his line because he could never choose where to fish. And even when he did stop he could not decide on whether to fish for salmon, halibut or rockfish. Needless to say, he was not a good provider for his family. They would have perished had it not been for Kingfisher.

"Kingfisher had watched the young man and decided it was time to teach him how to make decisions before his family starved. He flew down to the man and told him to watch and learn, then headed to his favourite perch on a tree overlooking the bay. There he sat, patiently watching for any ripple on the water. At the first sign, he plunged in and came up with a wriggling fish.

"Kingfisher returned to the man and said, 'You must find the courage to make decisions and stick with them. Choose one good place to fish and believe in yourself. Be patient, and have confidence that you have chosen well. Then, when a fish bites, pull it in.'"

Grandmother turned to the young woman and said, "Remember, like Kingfisher, to have the patience to take time and think about the decision you face. Then, find the courage and confidence in yourself to make your choice and stay with it."

Loon's Call

Long ago there was a young man who fell in love with a beautiful woman. They married and began a family together. Wherever one was, the other was always close by.

For the woman, life included the wonder of watching her children grow. She looked at the responsibilities of a family as a blessing, accepting that change was part of life. But the man did not. He missed the way things had been when he was young and carefree. He longed for those days to return.

Eventually he chose to leave his wife and family. He was sure, if he searched long enough, he would find the happiness he had lost. But each day he found only more loneliness. He wandered for days, until he could walk no longer. His strength ebbed like the flowing tide and with it went his pride. Finally, as he sat alone in the forest, he cried out for help.

From his perch on a nearby tree, Raven heard him and answered, "Don't worry, your family will soon be along to help you."

The man weakly replied, "No. They don't know where I am. I left them behind to go out and search for my happiness."

Raven was shocked. "Why did you leave the ones who love you?" he said. "No creature in this world is meant to survive alone. We all need each other. All you needed to do was look around you to find all the happiness you could ever want in the love of your family."

Raven could see the man growing weaker so he decided to make him a messenger to other people. He transformed him into Loon and gave him two calls. One is the sad wail we hear echoing across the lakes in the early morning—the call of a lonely soul. But the other call is the chuckling laugh we hear when Loon is with his family, enjoying the love and happiness they bring to life.

Quail's Family

Quail ran across the path in front of the girl and startled her. She felt her heart jump at the sudden appearance of the small bird. As the girl watched she saw another movement. Behind the mother were her little chicks, following along as if they were tied on a string.

The girl stopped and sat on an old log beside the path to watch. The family of birds ran about searching for food. They always kept together no matter what happened.

Watching Quail's family caused her to think about her own. When she, her brothers and sisters were young, they had followed her parents, just like the little chicks. She remembered the warm, secure feeling of always being close to those she loved.

But now her family was hardly ever together. Her parents were always busy, and her brothers and sisters had lives of their own. She began to cry and sobbed, "I wish my family could be together forever."

Quail, seeing her sadness, came over and began to talk to her. "Don't be sad that your family cannot be with you all the time. Use your memories of them to cheer you up. Look forward to and enjoy the times when you are together. When you grow up, share your love of family with your own children. That way they, too, will learn to build and value family ties."

The girl smiled and thanked Quail. As the tiny bird disappeared up the path with her chicks, the girl got up and headed down the path to her own home. She was determined to follow Quail's advice. From that day on, she would appreciate and cherish the joy that comes from being part of a loving family.

Raven Learns to Fly

Adaughter walked with her father along the beach at sunset. The young woman had only been married a few months, but already she and her husband had begun to have terrible arguments.

"Father," she said, "You and mother always seem to get along. How did you find so much happiness in your marriage?"

Father sat down with her on a log overlooking the bay. He said, "Love is a difficult thing to find and is even harder for two people to keep. It is like birds learning to fly. Even when they learn how to fly, they cannot stay aloft using only one wing.

"What should I do?" she asked.

Father replied, "Let me tell you the story of how Raven learned to fly, and perhaps it will help answer your question.

"When he was born, Raven could not fly. He had wings, but did not know how to use them. As each of his wings grew, feathers emerged; some short and strong, others long and supple. Raven would flap his right wing, then try his left, but he could not leave the ground and fly.

"One day when Eagle was soaring overhead, Raven called to her, 'I want to fly like you. Please teach me how.'

"Eagle replied, 'First you need to search and find the secret of flight.'

"So off Raven went, hopping along the ground on his short legs. He looked along the shoreline where the tide often brought treasures to the beach. He searched in the forest and on top of high mountains, but could not find the secret.

"After many days he returned to Eagle, very annoyed. Raven said, 'I have looked everywhere and I cannot find the secret of how to fly.'

"Eagle replied, 'You have taken a long journey. You have lifted rocks on the beach with one wing and used your other to help you climb the mountains. Your wings have grown strong. Now it is time for you to believe in their ability. You must let your wings work together and use their combined power for strong takeoffs. At the same time, you must allow each to be an individual, for it is the subtle differences in the spread of each feather and the angle of each tip that will enable you to gracefully fly among the trees of the forest.'

"Raven flapped his wings, but he was still hesitant. He perched on the edge of a cliff, fearful to try, but also afraid of missing his chance to fly. Finally, he spread his wings and slowly brought the tips together over his back. He leapt off the edge, swept his wings down, and soared into the sky.

"Raven loved to fly. He could feel the power of his wings working together, yet appreciated the job each one did in controlling his direction and path. Flying enabled him to set new goals and to turn his dreams into reality."

Father took his daughter's hand and said, "It is the same for us. As we grow from children to adults we spend a lot of time searching for the secret to love and how to keep it alive. Sometimes, like Raven, we take a long roundabout path only to find the answer has been with us all along.

"You and your husband need to be like Raven's wings. You need to allow each person to add their own special skills to help guide you along. But you also have to work together, because even Raven and Eagle cannot soar using only one wing."

Orca's Story

The rolling waves came up the channel and met the beach with a thundering roar. They picked up the stones and tumbled them against each other, slowly grinding them into pebbles and sand.

A family walked along the beach, enjoying the warm sun and the salty mist from the waves. Every so often one of the adults picked up a stone, carried it for a few minutes, dropped it, then picked up another.

The children were collecting handfuls of special rocks and running to give them to their mother and father. Their parents' pockets soon became full of stones to take home.

Later that day the family stopped at the grandparents' house. The children gathered around Grandfather and showed him their special rocks from the beach.

The old man held the stones in his hand for a long while. Then, he asked the children to gather in the cool shade of a big maple tree and he told them Orca's story.

"Many years ago the people of the world collected up all the stones from the beaches, built a pond, and filled it with water from the sea. They captured Orca, the whale, and held her in their stone pond for their own amusement. The people knew it was wrong to have such a noble whale captive, but they did not let her go.

"Orca longed to race through the open ocean and be able to leap into the warm summer air. She wanted to dive deep into the cold depths and chase fish. But in the small pond all she could do was swim in circles. Without her freedom, Orca knew she would never be happy.

"One day, Orca thought up a plan to escape. She began to swim faster and faster around the pond, creating a huge wave. When it grew so large that it almost touched the clouds, Orca leapt into the sky and became the crest of the great wave. The wave hit the pond's stone wall, smashed it down and rushed out into the sea.

"Now, Orca lives free, far out in the ocean. Each day she races through the sea, creating waves that crash onto the shore, slowly turning the stones into sand. Someday, she hopes all the stones will be gone and people will never again be able to build a pond to hold her captive."

Grandfather handed the stones back to the children. "That is why your beach stones feel special. Each one holds the energy of all the waves Orca has made, trying to turn it into sand."

Salmon's Spirit

It was late fall and the trees had lost most of their leaves. The cold water of the stream flowed over the stones and tumbled into pools along its way to the sea. In the quiet water along the banks, shadows were broken by the dart of a fish shooting up and through the rapids. Salmon had returned once again to spawn the next generation.

People had also come to the stream. Each year they looked forward to catching enough fish to feed their families through the winter. These people were careful and thoughtful about how many fish they took from the stream. They knew Salmon was a gift of Nature.

A child helped his father carry some fish up to their camp. He asked, "Why should we leave any fish in the river? If we take them all we will have lots to eat this winter. Besides, the ones we leave behind only live a few more days and then they die."

The father walked with his son over to their campfire and told him the story of Salmon's spirit. "When Nature first gave us this gift of food to help us through the long, cold winter, she also gave us the responsibility to care for Salmon. Even though the fish we do not take die after spawning, their spirits go to live in special stones in the stream. Those spirit stones protect Salmon's eggs until the small fish grow big enough to swim down to the sea."

The boy's father put another stick on the fire and continued the story. "When Salmon has grown up out in the ocean, it is the spirit stones that call them back to the stream where they were born. There, Salmon lay their eggs and then they, too, become spirit stones.

"That is why we always take care not to catch too many. For without the spirit stones to call them back, Salmon would not return each year to help feed us through the winter."

Seal

The water was calm as the man paddled his canoe across the bay. Overhead, Eagle soared on the midday wind, while at the edge of the woods Raven rested in a tree. Both watched the man.

They knew the man had a terrible fear of the sea. He longed to dive into it and swim but could not overcome his fear of drowning.

Raven and Eagle watched the man return to the village. They saw he lacked confidence in himself. His house was small because he was not sure he could build a larger one. He did not cook his food for fear he would burn it. In games, the man did not run as fast as he could in case he tripped.

Raven said, "How will he ever succeed?"

"He needs to discover the hidden talents that he holds within," Eagle replied.

"How can we help him?" Raven asked.

"We must choose our moment carefully," said Eagle. "Only when he loses his fear of failing will he discover the joy of success."

A few days later while the man was fishing with his children, a wave washed his young daughter overboard. Without thinking the man dove into the sea after her. In that instant Raven and Eagle transformed him into Seal. He saved his daughter and brought her safely to shore.

From that day onward, the man could transform himself into Seal whenever he wanted. As Seal, he could not only swim, but could swoop and dive in a world no other person had experienced. Now he looked forward to trying new things.

Raven and Eagle were happy. They knew his lesson would be shared with others. For just like the man, all of us have special talents just waiting to be transformed from dreams into reality, if only we have the courage to try.

Seasons

Winter was coming. Each day was shorter and cooler. Bright yellow autumn leaves sailed down out of the maple trees and carpeted the ground.

A family walked together down a pathway through the trees. There was a mother with her newborn child in her arms, a boy who would soon be an adult, the father in his middle years and two elder grandparents.

As they walked, a flight of geese flew overhead, heading south towards the sun.

One of the children said, "I'm cold. I wish it could always be summer."

The group stopped to build a fire to warm themselves. Grandfather sat and watched the geese disappearing into the distance and then began to tell a story.

"Long ago there were no seasons," he said. "We all lived every day in a world that never changed. It never got warmer, it never got colder. Every day was the same as the one before and the one to come. Our elders decided we should follow the geese to see if they could help us find a place where life would be different. As we followed them south, we found warm summer days, with plenty of fresh food and many happy times.

"When we went north we found cold winter days, little food and many hardships. Some of the people wanted to go back to the time when there was no change, but our elders knew change was good. They had learned from following the geese the importance of seasons. They knew you could only really enjoy a warm day if you had experienced a cold one."

Grandfather looked at his grandson and said, "Just like the seasons, life is full of change. We all go through good times and bad times. Some people wish every day could bring only happiness. But remember, it is the few sad days we experience that allow us to appreciate all the happy ones."

Teacher

Raven soared high in the early morning sky, surveying the world below. She watched the deer emerging from the forest into the meadow to feed on grass frosted with dew. On the beach she saw kingfishers hovering over the water, then diving into the shallow lagoon to catch eels and sculpins. On the reef she saw otters slink between the rocks, looking for crabs and clams. The surface of the bay rippled with herring being chased by seals.

Raven enjoyed watching these creatures teach their young to hunt and find food. She saw the doe nuzzle aside the coarse grass and show her fawn the tender shoots hidden below. The kingfishers gave their young a demonstration on how to surprise their catch with a quick dive from above. Otters coaxed their pups to explore crevices to find hidden food. She watched a colony of seals show their pups how to work together to herd herring into dense schools.

Raven said to herself, "All the wise creatures of the world show their young the many important things they need to know. I want to teach the children all about the things I know, for I have had many adventures and learned many lessons."

Raven searched for some way to get her message to the children. One day, she came upon a storyteller. "You have a special gift," she said, "for you have heard my stories and can share them with the children. You will be Teacher."

Raven said to Teacher: "Take the children down life's pathway, starting every morning from the point you stopped the night before. Show the children how to solve puzzles, the way deer in the meadow find the tender grass. Teach them to study a problem, then make a decision, the way kingfishers hover then strike. Demonstrate the benefits of searching and discovering hidden treasures along their path, like otters search among the rocks of the reef. And teach them to work together, the way seals herd herring in the bay."

"Every morning I will fly over the forest to call the children and bring them to you. I will protect them from harm by wrapping them in my wings. The young children will be in the small feathers closest to my breast, the older ones will be among the long feathers at the tips."

To this day, Raven can be heard flying high in the morning sky, her wings whispering to children to wake up and learn more lessons about life. Then Teacher takes and guides them another few steps along the path—exploring, discovering, making decisions, and working together.

Otter Play

The woman was always in a hurry. Each day seemed busier than the one before and there was always a long list of things that needed to be done.

One day her husband took her up to the meadow behind their home. As they sat, he pointed out the new buttercups shining in the sunlight, the smell of the dry grass waving in the wind, and the laughter of their children playing on the beach. They saw an otter family playing hide and seek among the boulders on the reef. The woman realized it was the first time in months that she had noticed those things.

"I have no time to enjoy life," she said. "I'm always too busy to stop and see what's going on around me. I wish I had time to play."

Her husband thought about what she had said. He took her hand: "Otter once had the same problem. Let me tell you her story.

"Many years ago Otter learned that life was too short to fill with nothing but tasks. Instead, she chose to take a playful attitude towards things she had to do.

"Now when she is searching for food, she turns it into a game of hide and seek with her children. They dash along the sand, splash in the surf and scramble among the stones in an explosion of energy and curiosity. When it is hot they swim in the cool ponds or lie in the shade, watching clouds drift by.

"Sometimes Otter does things just for fun, nothing more. A grassy bank is turned into a slippery slide or a shallow bay becomes the scene of a frenzied game of tag.

"But there is still time to be serious. When it comes to important things, like protecting her family, she focuses all her energy on that. But when she is done, she takes time to enjoy her children and discover the grace and beauty of the world around her.

The husband looked at his wife. "Remember, our children will grow up and our lives will pass whether you are watching or not.

"Take time now to enjoy the view from where you are. Study the beauty of a single flower or the color of sunlight coming through leaves of a tree. Listen to the sound of the ocean's waves crashing onto the shore. Feel the wind and wonder where it's been. Taste the flavour of wild berries just picked from the vine. Enjoy the comfort of loved ones close by."

They walked down to the shoreline, and for the first time in years she ran with her children on the beach, feeling the cool sand on the soles of her feet. She splashed in the waves and lay on the warm rocks, watching the birds fly by. She took a long walk with her husband and sat with him by the campfire telling stories to her children. She found all the happiness and contentment her heart could ever want playing with her family and enjoying nature's gifts.

Wolf's Wilderness

The evening was cool. It was fall and the family were preparing for the cold, dark nights of the coming winter. As they sat around their campfire, bathed in its warm light, they heard the distant howl of Wolf.

One of the children said, "Wolf sounds so sad. I wonder why?"

Mother replied, "Wolf is calling for something he lost long ago."

"What did he lose?" asked her son.

Mother said, "Let me tell you the story of Wolf's wilderness. It will help you to understand Wolf's sad howl.

"Long ago, Wolf and people lived together as one family. There was lots of food, and it was shared among all the creatures in the valley.

"One winter the snow fell so deep that it was difficult for the people to find enough food. Wolf said to the people, 'I can run over the snow better than you, so I will travel to the next valley and stay there until spring. That will leave the food here for you.'

"And so Wolf left that valley and went to stay in the wilderness on the other side of the mountain. But when spring came, the people were afraid there might not be enough food the next winter, so they sent a message telling Wolf not to come back.

"Eventually, the people used up all Nature's gifts in their valley so they moved into Wolf's wilderness and forced him to move into the next valley."

Mother took the boy's hand as they listened to Wolf's distant cry from the mountain. She said, "Now almost all of the valleys are gone. Wolf has no place to go and people are still not willing to share. That is why today we hear Wolf's sad howl echoing through the valleys he used to call home."

Mother looked at her son. "It is now up to us to listen to Wolf and find a way to live in harmony again with him and all the wilderness creatures. If we don't, it will soon be us crying for the home we have lost."

Tree Frog

The cool evening breeze made it feel good to sit around the warm campfire. As darkness fell, the sound of tree frogs began to come from the forest.

A child, cuddled up to his grandmother, asked, "Why do the frogs in the forest chirp so loud?"

Grandmother smiled at him. She said, "They have to because it is very hard to wake up Maple Tree when she is sleeping."

"How come Maple Tree is sleeping?" the little one asked.

As the campfire glowed, she answered by telling the story of Tree Frog.

"Many, many years ago, before any of us were born, all the plants in the world could make music. Every day the world was full of songs coming from choirs of towering trees and fields of flowers.

"The most beautiful voice was that of Maple Tree. When bright sunlight shone down and lit up her leaves she would sing a song so beautiful that every-one would stop and listen. As long as the sun shone, Maple Tree would keep up her sweet chorus."

"One day when the sun set, a cold winter darkness came. All of Maple Tree's leaves turned brown and fell to the ground. Without them, she could no longer make music.

"The birds in the forest decided to help. They gathered up her withered leaves and flew with them high up into the winter sky and let them go. As each leaf drifted down and touched the earth, it became a small tree frog. Each frog was the same bright green color as sunlight shining through Maple Tree's leaves.

"Now, in the spring of every year, Tree Frog starts to call to Maple Tree. As the nights get warmer, Tree Frog chirps louder and louder until Maple Tree finally wakes up. Then, she stretches her long branches into the sky, and gives birth to a new set of bright green leaves."

The child looked up and asked, "How come Maple Tree doesn't sing any more?"

"Oh, but she does," Grandmother replied. "If you lie very quietly under Maple Tree on a warm summer day, you can hear her. It may sound like wind whisper-ing through leaves but it is actually Maple Tree turning the sunlight into music."

Matchmaker

Long ago in different villages by the sea, a young boy and girl grew into adults. Raven and Eagle knew the two would be perfect mates.

Unfortunately, the paths taken by the young man and woman seldom crossed. He was an artist who spent his days in the forest searching for images to use in his carvings. She was a storyteller who stayed in her village teaching children.

Raven and Eagle devised a plan to bring them together. They enticed each of them to take walks along the beach at night. It was a good plan, and would have worked except that in those days there was no light in the night sky. Every evening the two lovers-to-be passed in the dark, neither knowing the other was there.

Raven said, "I will find a torch and hold it up in the sky so that they will be able to see each other."

That night Raven entered a camp and stole a burning log from the fire. It was considerably heavier than he had expected. As he tried to fly away, it dragged along, leaving behind a bright streak of firelight on the surface of the sea. Eagle, seeing Raven's problem, came to his aid and using his strong wings helped lift the burning light high up into the night sky. There, it became a round glowing moon called Matchmaker.

When the man came down to the sea, he was drawn towards Matchmaker's light reflecting on the water. The young woman, starting from the other end of the beach, was also lured by the shimmering light. When the two met, they saw each other for the first time and, illuminated by Matchmaker's soft light, fell instantly in love.

Raven and Eagle were very pleased. Ever since then they have kept the moon fire burning so that when lovers walk by the sea at night, they can still share Matchmaker's glow sparkling on the water.

About the Author

Born in Vancouver, British Columbia, in 1953, Robert James (Jim) Challenger lives in Victoria, on the southern end of Vancouver Island.

Jim has spent his life absorbing all the stories the Northwest Coast has to offer. A keen observer of the natural behaviour of wildlife, he has developed his own style of artwork that captures the essence of the many creatures that live around him.

Jim is an accomplished artist and stone carver, and has sold his beach-stone and glass carvings to collectors around the world. His highly sought-after form-line designs capture the shape and movement of his subjects while maintaining the simplicity of flowing lines and shapes.

Jim's stories and designs bring a unique perspective to how we can learn from nature's examples in the world that surrounds us. For more information about the author, you can visit his website: http://www.rjchallenger.com